The Strange Ways of Dragons

An Allegory

By

Arthur Lee Conway

Other books by the same author

Walking through the Mist of Life
The Poetic Vibrations of a Matured Butterfly

ISBN: 979-8-9866193-0-9 (e)

ISBN: 979-8-9866193-1-6 (sc)

Reprint

Printed in the United States of America

Illustrations by Arthur Lee Conway

Dedicated to Walter Conway, Jr. 1927 – 1984

*A mere mortal whose marathon like Will caused him to
become a true Dragonslayer*

Table of Contents

Once upon a time in some common , typical place in the world of Now, a little colorless Boy closed his eyes to escape from the land of Hearsay, his mind had become weak after being constantly bombarded by disinformation. Slowly, robotic-like, he drifted away and ventured into the land of Awareness. There he met an old Sage that sat upon the very air, at least it seemed so; the hoary Sage was mumbling something, it sounded like a religious chant. The Boy thought it to be nothing more than gibberish, but he was too faraway to really hear anything. Not until he came closer to himself, and allowed his inner being to hear, listen to the Sage's mystical voice… surprisingly, he began to understand what was truthfully being said.

The small man kept repeating something about a Dragon, a fierce Dragon, no, not just one Dragon, but many Dragons.

"Dragons, what's so special… so evil about Dragons?" asked the colorless Boy.

"Dragons are fomenters of mankind ills, little Boy," replied the Sage.

"How can that be so, old Man?" asked the Boy.

"Rest little boy of the mind, and I'll tell you about the devious ways of Dragons. But, you must open yourself, your mind to the world of Nothingness," said the Sage.

Dragons were created by the God

And Goddess of Want....

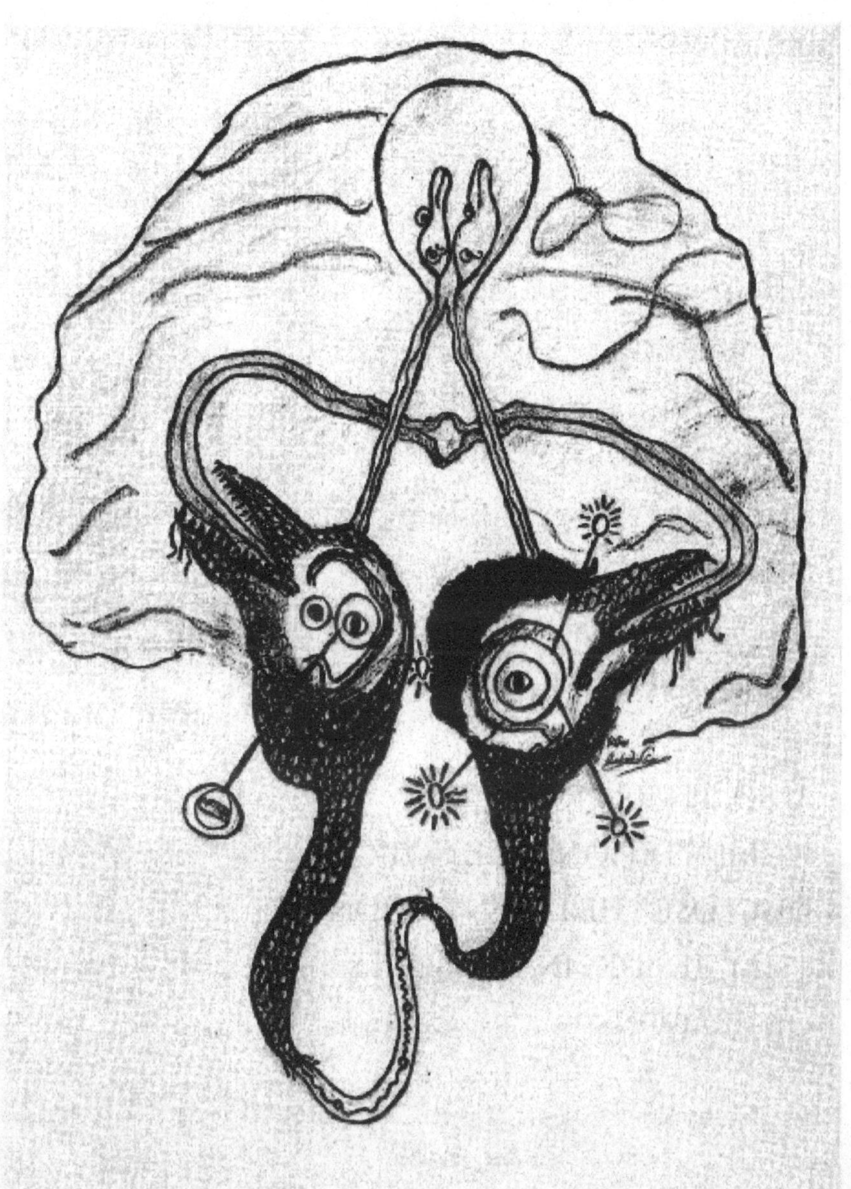

WARNING!

DRAGONS CANNOT
BE DISTINGUISHED
BY THEIR COLOR...

ALSO, THEIR PROFOUND
PIGMENTATION WILL NOT
DISCLOSE THE LATENT MADNESS
THAT RESIDES IN THE SOULS
OF DRAGONS.

A Dragon's eye can see
beyond the expansive sight
of the eagle in flight.

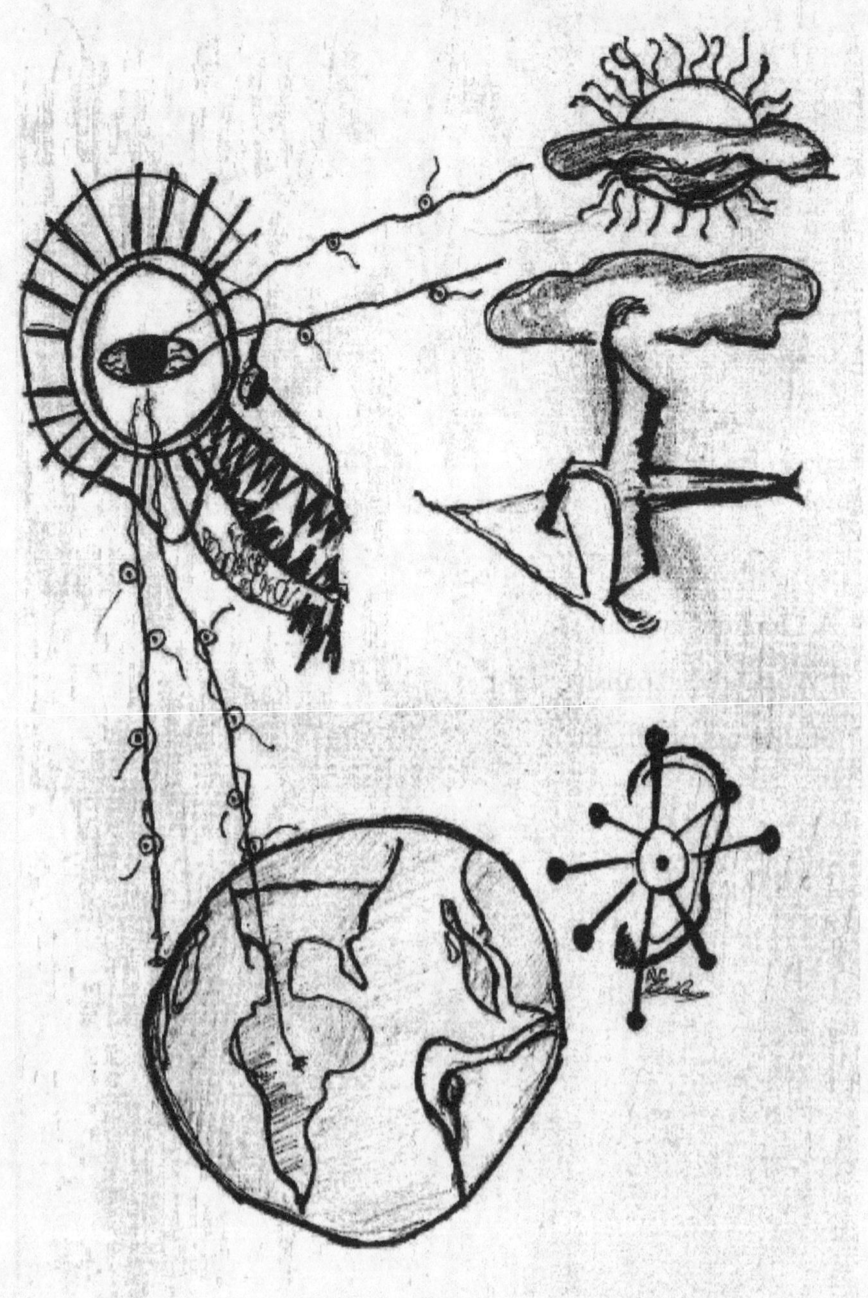

Dragon ears are larger, more aware
of the Mythholders presence
than all of Nature's elephant
ears put together.

Dragons come in all sizes,
but nevertheless, they usually
come to conquer all mirages
of Nations that belittle themselves.

Some Dragons are cute
and cuddly, causing the Mythholders
to melt in their sentimental
Minds of self-foolery,
until they realize the terror
that lies within,

SEE

how hard and difficult
it is to get along with the Dragons
of NO SOUL...
without sacrificing ,
paying with their own soul.

Dragons are edible,
but it takes a mentally
strong Stomach to digest
its rancid flesh.

Dragons love control,
total control,
total control of the Mythholders movement,
or they will die.

Dragons
are
excessively
greedy.

Converted Dragons are more treacherous,

MORE TREACHEROUS,

MORE TREACHEROUS,

than hereditary Dragons,

for

BANKRUPTCY

in the financial

PLAYGROUNDS OF THE WORLD

could

mean

a

total

demise

of

their very

existence.

Oftentimes, Dragons can be found wading

around in lakes of Personal Hell…

inviting common, adaptable

Mythholders to join them

for a swim in the same hellish waters.

Some

     Dragons

         are

            known

               to

                  become

DESTRUCTIVELY sick,

when other Dragons of equal stature,

decline to wallow in their sloppy

puddles of ancient idealism

of total Erde reform.

Dragons
can be like Andre Maginot
Line of invincibility…

deceiving
to
those
Beings
that
develop
a
dependency
upon
it.

Dragons believe in Liberalism
in times of progress.

The Dragon will make you pay for his MEAL
and your own MEAL… and won't
hesitate to SCREAM BLOODY MURDER, or TREASON,
if you decline to do so,

or if you attempt to lick your fingers
and try to grab an EXTRA CRUMB,

yet, a Dragon will take the whole plate right
before your very eyes.

Words

Watch the Dragon that prophesy,
speaks of future prosperity,
when he knows well like other mythological
Beings of former times, that fornicated in the septic
pools… Industrial Palaces of Maya, that the power
of clairvoyance exist in no one, except in the creatures of Agape.

Dragons are very selfish,

they will not share the light

of Gnosis

with anyone,

except with other Dragons,

but sometimes certain Dragons

refuse to share the fire

of Gnosis with their own

Dragon cronies;

in fear,

that a kernel of Awareness

on the part

of other Dragons about

various subtle & peculiar

acts of intrigue,

might be used

against their power

on any given day of Dragon vengeance.

The Dragon will
combat Truth
with hot Rhetoric.

The Dragon will show no sympathy
for Mythholders...

when the Leash of Prosperity becomes
a Noose of Economical death.

The Dragon love to fornicate…
he will copulate with his sister,
daughter, mother,
other Dragons' wives,

Dragons love to penetrate
Minds and Lives,
and any Mythholder

for doing likewise.

A
Dragon
Will
Screw
His
Mother
For
A
Slice
Of
MORTAL
glory.

Dragons are myths out of the past,

DRAGONS ARE MYTHS OUT OF THE PAST…

returning only in times of despair.

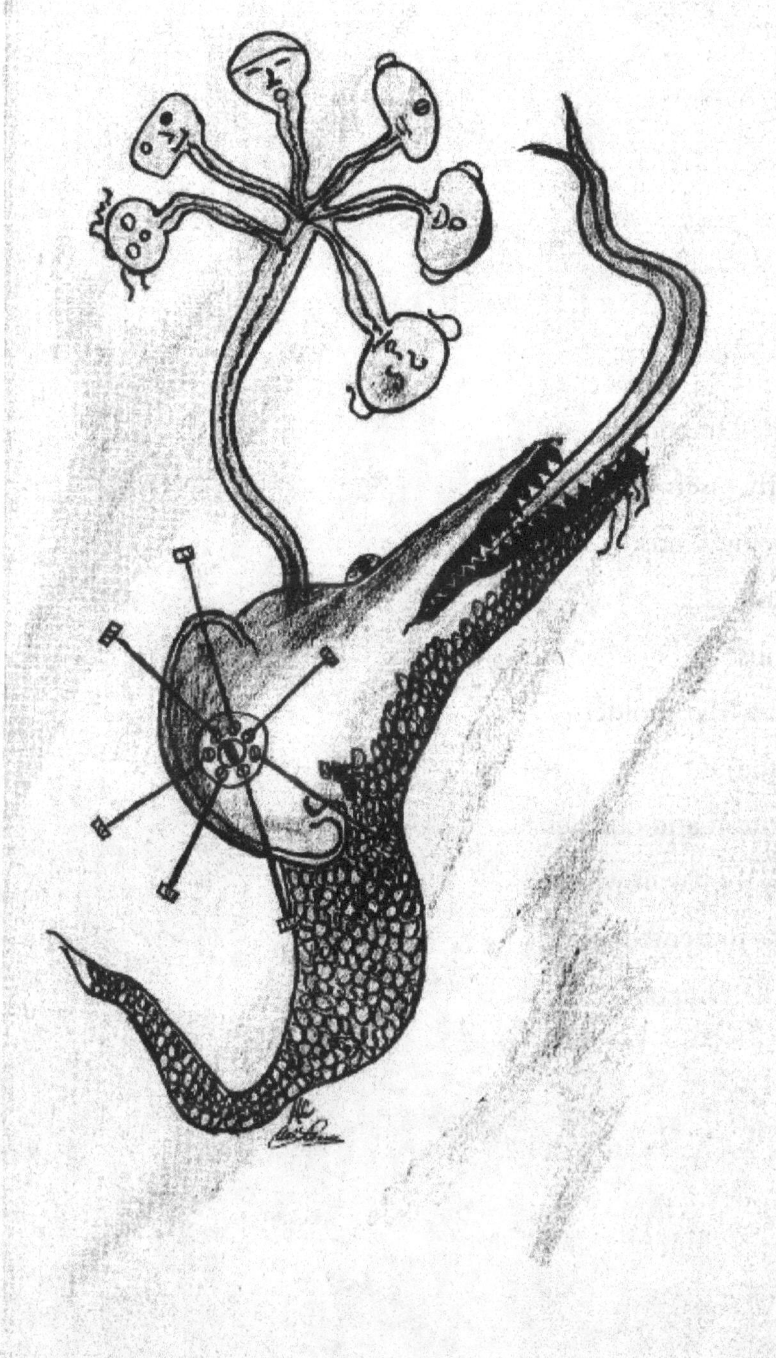

Some Dragons
see themselves
as being Gods,
mainly
because
of the Mythholders
profound
devotion and obedience
to every pagan whim
that's presented
by the Dragons.

MOST DRAGONS LOVE TO EAT minds,

many

Dragons

consider

it

a

delicacy.

Dragons are known to feast upon apathy
like that legendary creature of Transylvania
fed upon the blood of countless

unsuspecting females.

A Dragon will latch
onto a Mythholders' head
like a leech sucking
blood for survival.

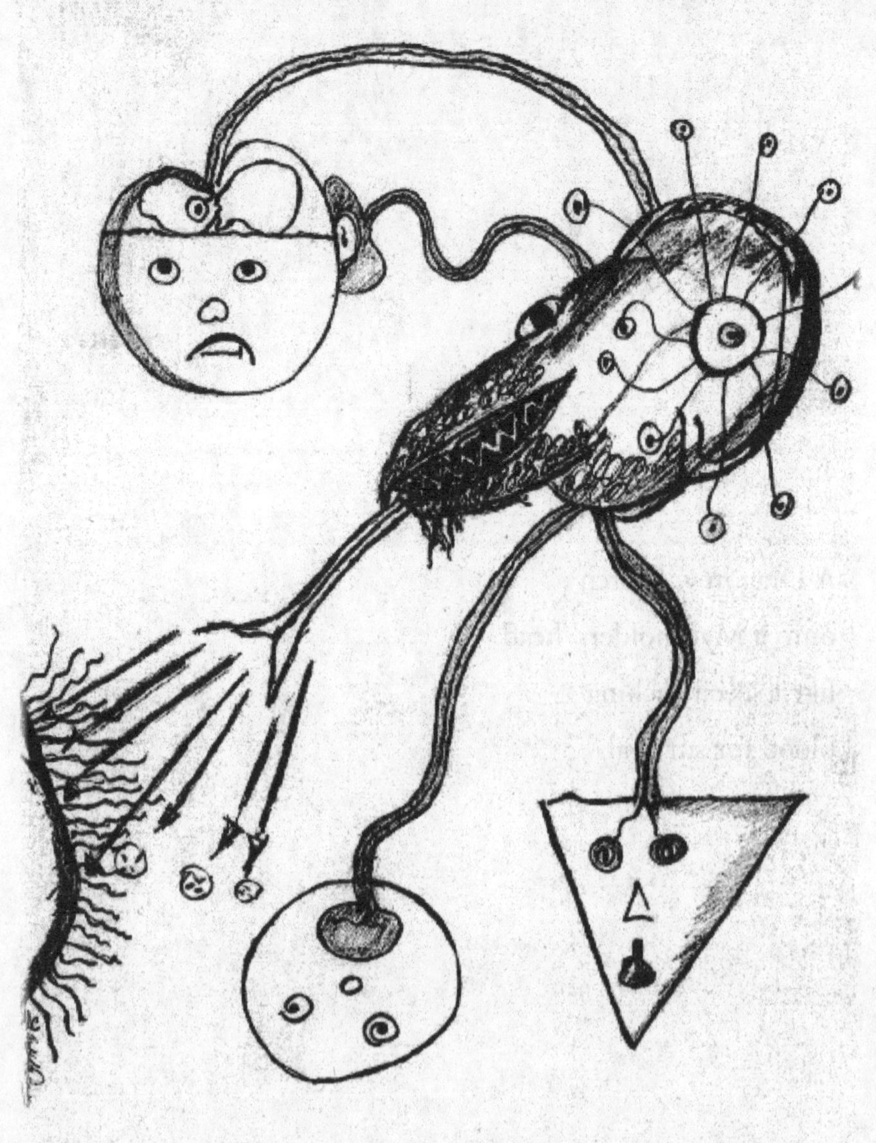

Some Dragons
can be found
with large empty heads
standing on medieval
corners
playing a game
called *Nothing*.

The Dragon will come
in the Mindwomb
of a Mythholder,
and will leave only
after it has been confirmed,
that a Mythholders' mental
egg is completely fertile.

Dragon women are known to drive cold,
emotionless stakes of verbiage through the hearts
of mothers and children of destitution…
without showing even a twitch of pity in their harden faces.

Dragons will

promise you something,

promise you something,

PROMISE YOU SOMETHING,

until you die waiting

SEE, Dragons are masters of sophistry.

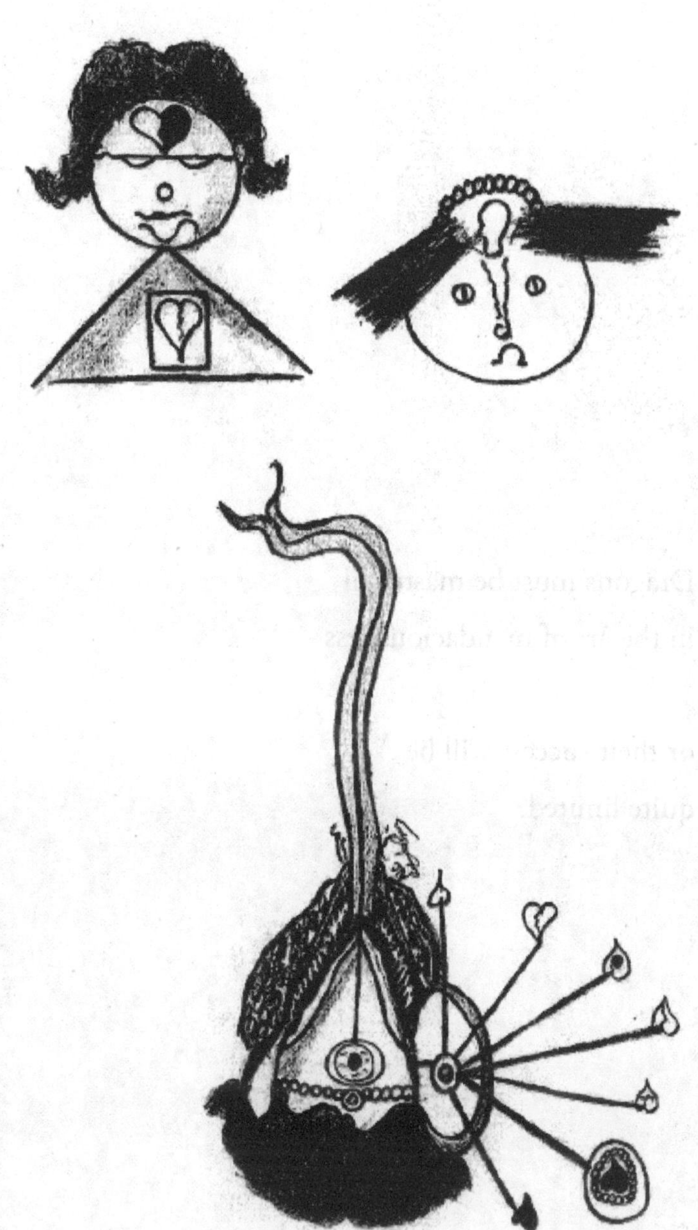

Dragons must be masterful
in the art of mendaciousness

or their success will be
quite limited.

Some Dragons can be found
wearing cloaks of permanent
Opprobrium,

when allowed to participate, given
exclusive, honored rights;

indulge in various playful, but life
supporting activities within the smaller
playgrounds of Nations.

Dragons often play dice
with the future of other Nations
as bargaining chips,

laughing when they
crap out
with a Nation's life.

Like a chameleon changing
colors, blending with Nature's surrounding,
so do Dragons often re-color
their empty hearts,
and will attempt, sacrifice their own
children like Abrahams' rendering of Isaac,

motivated by sightless faith,

yes, Dragons will make
un-thoughtful bargains
just to be caressed by Materialism
feverish hands.

The dragon's guardians
will drag dark of mind individuals away,

into deeper internal darkness.

BEWARE OF THE DRAGONS' GUARDIANS.

Once a Dragon realizes that the mood
of a Mythholder has started to drift away,
drift away, drift away,

float pass blind patriotism, and wanton nationalism,

a Dragon will react insanely violent,

just to recapture that transformative mindset of the Mythholder.

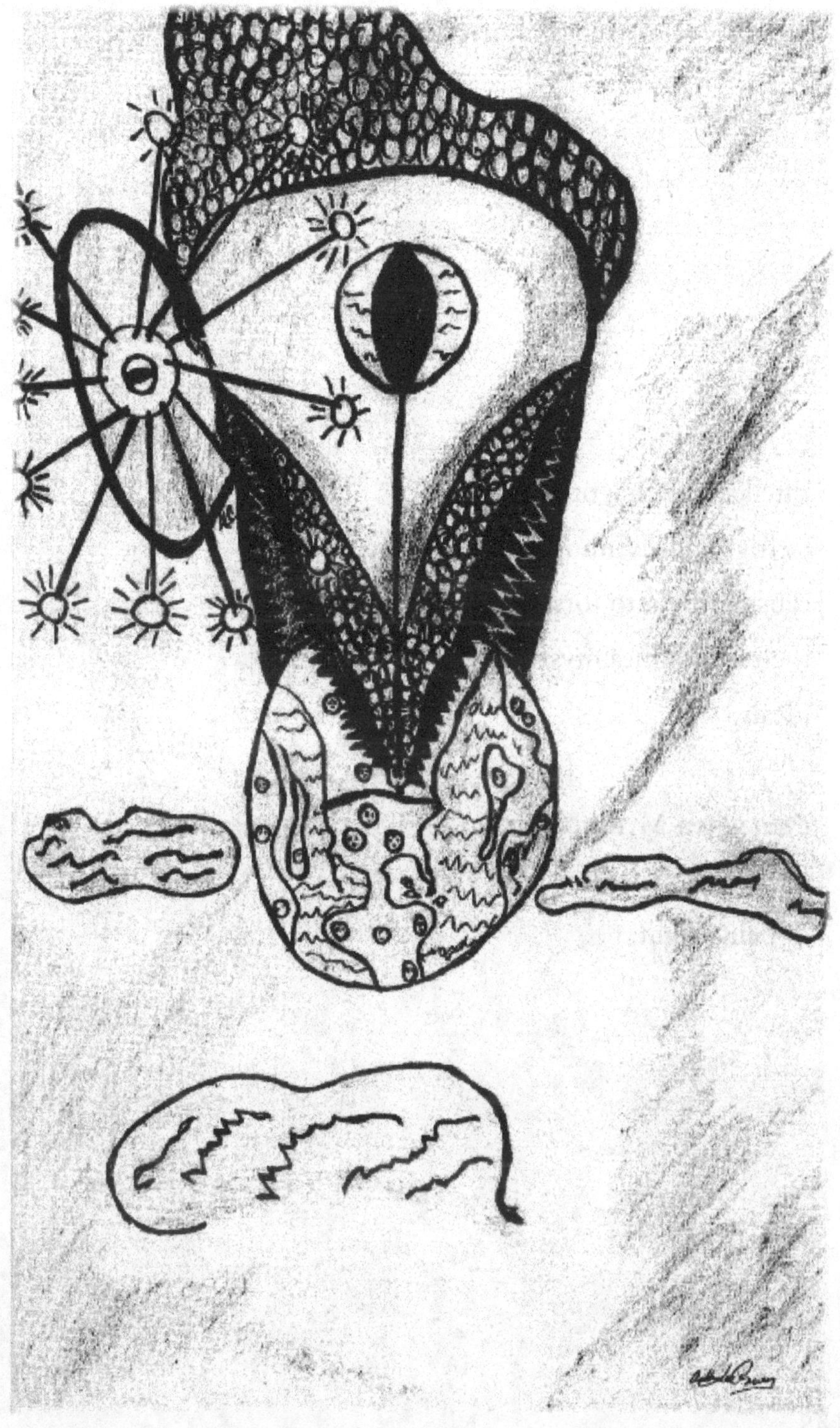

Intellectual Dragons tend
to frighten Mythholders;
causing them to forsake
their oftentimes mystical
ideals,

even when Mythholders
harbor strong convictions
of being right.

In times of fierce fighting
most Dragons will not be found
in the heat of battle,

but,

Dragons love that aromatic smell of Deaths' pleasures.

The Dragon will readily exterminate
another Race with economical fire,
just to ease his ulcerous greed.

Dragons cannot stand smelling old
Bones.

Dragons will attack Dragons,

Dragons will attack Dragons,

DRAGONS WILL ATTACK DRAGONS…

when reincarnated Dragons

go into the mind dens of Mythholders,

and attempt to destroy the cancerous beliefs

of the Mythholders; that Dragons are mystical.

Watch out for Dragons
in your own home,

they will eat the nutrients of survival hardily,
love your mind and body lustily,

enjoy your presence truly,

but can be found traveling in Dragon coaches of intrigue,
secretly, madly killing you,

while quietly watching your Soul melt away
without batting an eye in sorrow.

BEWARE OF THE DRAGONS IN YOUR OWN HOME.

Praise Lord Dragon,
Praise lord Dragon,
and when Salvation
closes its doors on you.

Praise Lord Dragon
for your misfortunes.

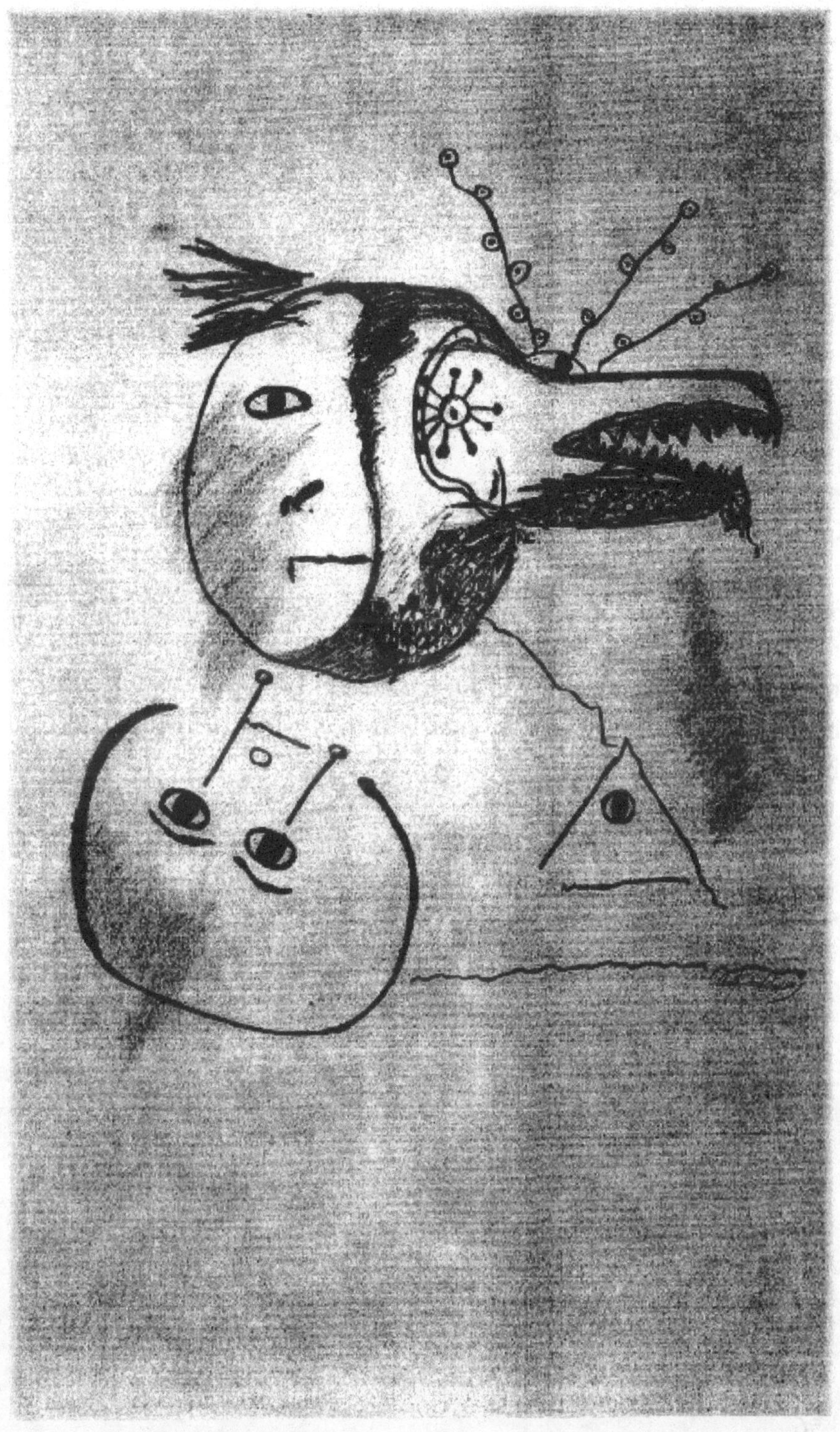

"Everything must die, destroy its wanton, worldly self, and reclaim its Child-Self…even Dragons," said the old Sage. As the colorless Boy started to open his eyes slowly, like before his journey into the world of Dragons.

About the Author

ARTHUR LEE CONWAY is a native of Charlottesville, Virginia, and has attended the University of Maryland University College, graduating with an A.A. in Business Administration.

He is the author of WALKING THROUGH THE MIST OF LIFE, THE STRANGE WAYS

OF DRAGONS, and has written his third book: THE POETIC VIBRATIONS OF A MATURED BUTTERFLY: POEMS AND PARABLES. Winner of a 2018 Summer Pinnacle Book Achievement Award. 2021 Literary Titan Book Gold Award winner for Poetry.

You can contact him at:

Arthur Conway

PO. BOX 90328

Washington, DC 20090